E   A 92-167
Hol   Hollingsworth, Mary

           Christmas in Happy
Forest

		DATE DUE	

GOD'S
Happy
FOREST

CHRISTMAS IN HAPPY FOREST

Love Is the Greatest Gift

Written by
Mary Hollingsworth

Illustrated by
Mary Grace Eubank

Story Concept by
Charlotte Greeson

Brownlow

Brownlow Publishing Company, Inc.

In memory of Joy Samson,
fondly known as
"Josephine Elizabeth Orangeblossom,"
who lived on "Plumb-and-Nearly Lane
(plumb out of town
and nearly in the country)"
— a loving teacher and good friend.

Dear Parents and Teachers:

Everyone likes to give and receive gifts, especially at Christmas. And the best gifts of all are gifts of the heart. Ask a mother whether she would rather have a fancy arrangement of flowers from a florist with a formal card or a clump of dusty daisies handed to her with a crooked, five-year-old smile. Ask a dad whether he would prefer a silk shirt and tie or a rough-hewn shoe shine box his son made for him in shop class at school. It's the amount of heart a gift contains that makes it special.

Christmas in Happy Forest teaches children that (1) love is the greatest gift they can offer to others and (2) that giving can be more fun than getting. The animal children in this gentle story of love learn these valuable lessons from their grumpy teacher, Miss Orangeblossom. Through their kindness to her, they see love turn her grumpiness to gladness, loneliness to laughter and frustration to friendship.

Love can truly change the world, and can change us. Why not share *Christmas in Happy Forest* with a child now and laugh at the happy ending?

The Publisher

Miss Josephine Liz'beth Orangeblossom was the school teacher in Happy Forest's one-room schoolhouse. She lived in a giant tree trunk out on Plumb-and-Nearly Lane. (It was *plumb* out of Happy Forest and *nearly* in the deep, dark woods.)

#1
PLUMB AND
NEARLY LANE
ORANGEBLOSSOM

None of the kids liked Miss Orangeblossom. She was a stern, little-old-lady raccoon who wore wire glasses. Miss Orangeblossom was as stiff and proper as she could be. She was always grouchy and never smiled.

Today was the last day of school before Christmas. Bennie Beaver was helping Miss Orangeblossom carry her big, heavy books to school as usual. He didn't like it, but he did it. "Be careful, Bennie. And don't be so slow!" she fussed.

In spite of Miss Orangeblossom's scolding, Bennie was excited. Today was the day for the all-school Christmas party. They would have freshly picked berries, mixed forest nuts and delicious wild grapes. And they would all trade presents.

But then something terrible happened. As they walked
up the steps of the school Miss Orangeblossom fell.

"Oophs, OUCH, oh no!" she cried as she tumbled
down the slippery steps. "I've hurt my ankle!"

Creeper Turtle started to laugh. Bennie frowned at him
and then bent down to help Miss Orangeblossom up. Prickles
Porcupine began picking up her books and glasses.

Because Miss Orangeblossom couldn't
walk, Scamper and Scurry, the twin squirrels,
helped her home. As she left, Bennie tried
to be nice by saying,
"Merry Christmas."

"Merry Christmas?" roared the teacher. "It's going to be a *terrible* Christmas. I won't be able to go to my nephew's house. And I certainly don't have any friends in this miserable, lonely forest!"

You could hear her still mumbling as she limped out of sight.

"Hooray!" shouted Creeper Turtle, "No school today!"
He didn't really care that grouchy Miss Orangeblossom was
hurt. But wait, no school today meant no Christmas party.

Oh no!

"Well, isn't that just like her," complained Waddles the Duck. "She up and gets hurt the last day before Christmas just so we can't have our party. She's such an old grouch."

"But, she didn't used to be that way," said a quiet voice suddenly from the doorway. Then in stepped Prickles.

Swifty Rabbit asked, "How do you know that?"
Prickles sat down on a nearby desk. "I used to live
in Sleepy Valley," she said sadly. "And
Miss Orangeblossom was my
teacher there, too.

She was the happiest, most wonderful teacher in the whole world then."

"What happened to her?" asked Daisy Skunk.

"There was a big fire in Sleepy Valley," said Prickles. "The school burned down. All my friends were burned out. We lost our house in the fire."

"My mom says that Miss Orangeblossom's house burned in the fire, too. She lost everything she had."

"Oh, that's terrible," said Bennie. "Then what happened?"

"We all had to find new places to live."

"Miss Orangeblossom had to move to Happy Forest. This was the only school that needed a teacher. But her friends and family moved to Honey Grove on the other side of the deep, dark woods."

"We didn't know that," said Waddles quietly.

"Boy, I feel terrible for laughing at her," said Creeper. "Maybe Miss Orangeblossom has been grouchy because she's been sad and lonely."

"Yeah," said Bennie. "She just needs some friends to cheer her up."

"Hey, I've got a great idea!" said Swifty Rabbit. They all gathered around as Swifty whispered a secret to each one of them. Then, bright-eyed and laughing, they scampered off into Happy Forest.

The next day was Christmas Eve. The children scurried about excitedly. As they passed each other in the forest, they whispered and giggled. Each one was busy with a really important assignment.

At sunset the kids met in front of Miss Josephine Liz'beth Orangeblossom's house. They worked quietly for several minutes near the little fir tree just outside her bedroom window.

Then Bennie Beaver went over
to the window. He thumped on it
softly with his big, flat tail. Slowly
Miss Orangeblossom's head poked out
the window. She was frowning, as usual.
"Oops," said Swifty, "I think we've made a
BIG mistake."

But then Miss Orangeblossom saw her little tree. Scamper and Scurry had made long strings of walnuts for it. A pretty, featherlined bird's nest from Twitter Redbird sat on one branch. Prickles had hung apples and pinecones on the limbs. And big clusters of fat, red berries hung all over the tree.

Bennie decided to try again. "Merry Christmas, Miss Orangeblossom," he said softly. And he handed her a wild-plum Christmas pudding he had made — her very favorite!

Wonder of wonders! A tiny twitch started at the edge of Miss Orangeblossom's mouth. And pretty soon, her whole mouth turned up into a big, beautiful smile!

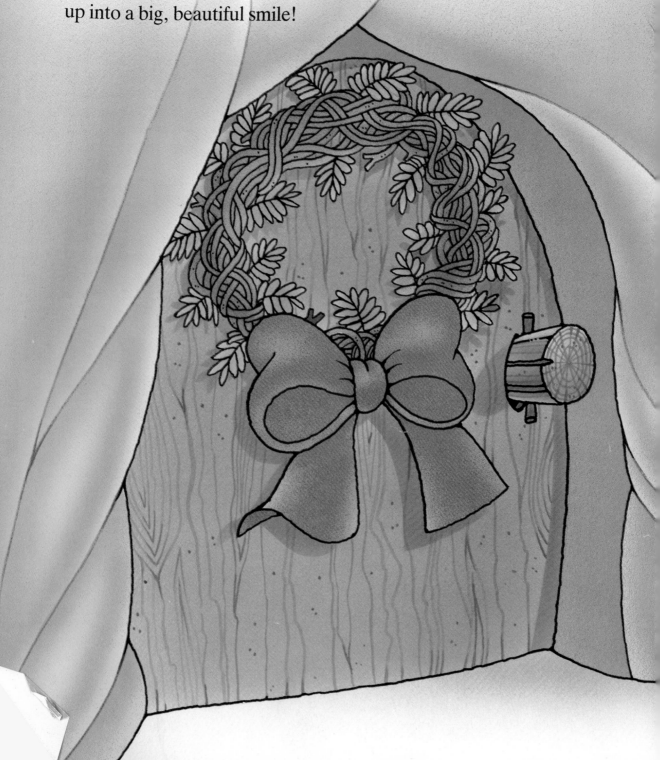

Just then marvelous snowflakes started to fall. They landed on the fir tree until it looked as if God himself had decorated it.

Suddenly, out of the dark woods came twinkling, starry lights. It was Freddie Firefly and his entire family. They flew around the top of the Christmas tree in a circle like a tiny, lighted halo. Gently, they landed all over the little tree, with Freddie on the very top.

Miss Orangeblossom said, "This is the most special Christmas I've ever had." And a big tear trickled down her face.

Then she said, "I'm sorry. I know I've been a grouch. But now I know I can have lots of friends right here in Happy Forest. I love each one of you." After that, Miss Orangeblossom smiled and laughed and hugged a lot. All her students thought she was the sweetest, best teacher they had ever had.

That's how everyone in Happy Forest learned the real secret of loving. Giving gifts to Miss Orangeblossom made *everyone* feel happy. They all realized that giving is even better than getting.